AF408881

Among Other Things

Börkur Sigurbjörnsson

Among Other Things
flash fiction

Urban Volcano

Among Other Things
Börkur Sigurbjörnsson

Creative Commons (BY-NC-ND) – 2024
https://creativecommons.org/licenses/by-nc-nd/4.0/

Cover: Ana Piñeyro

Illustrations: Börkur Sigurbjörnsson

Publisher: Urban Volcano

https://urbanvolcano.net/

ISBN 978-9935-9466-9-0

This book can be reproduced by any means one can think of, such as, but not limited to, photo-copying, chiseling into a limestone rock, or reading out-loud during a work-related Zoom conference call from a bathtub at midsummer solstice, provided that the author is referenced, the content is not modified, and the reproduction is not done commercially.

Contents

Among other things is a collection of flash fiction born from ideas that have surfaced in my mind over the past few years. To some extent, these narratives are part of a personal arts therapy journey where I reflect on my perception of the world, strive to understand it, and carve out my own space within it.

The collection doesn't have a specific overarching theme but some concepts that are particularly dear to me find their way into multiple stories, presenting repetitive scenarios where I explore these concepts from different angles.

I encourage you not to rush through the book in one sitting or feel compelled to read the stories in sequence. Instead, treat the collection as a companion to be revisited occasionally. Dip in from time to time and choose a couple of stories at random.

Paris, June 25th 2024
   Börkur Sigurbjörnsson

Dawn

The sun comes up from behind the mountain and its golden rays glitter on the lake at the bottom of the valley. The birds wake up and start singing as they fly from one branch to another, picking juicy berries for breakfast. The mice run along the timber railing throwing flakes of loose paint into the air as their tiny feet meet the worn-out and rotting timber. The foxes yawn, making their way from the edge of the woods into the fields to capture a bit of the heat from the rising sun. A black-tailed godwit roots around in the soil until it hits something hard. It pulls the object out on to the surface with its beak. A human bone. Possibly a part of a finger. The area is littered with the rotting remains of this extinct species.

Nobody knows exactly how the extinction came to be. Yet, theories are abundant. Some say it was a sort of auto-extinction or autoimmunity. Others point to natural disasters, volcanic eruptions, meteors, or even extra terrestrial beings. Nobody knows but everyone thinks they know.

The godwit lets the bone drop to the ground and turns on its concentration. It thinks the bone discovery conscientiously into the universal consciousness, before it flaps its wings and lifts itself into the air.

Happy ... Nothing!

Dear journal!

Dear myself!

To whoever it may or may not concern.

Thought of Jo this morning. Facebook told me it was his birthday. Found it ideal to send him a line. We've lost contact after going our separate ways after our studies in Berlin. We who connected so well in those days. The relationship was somehow so effortless. Like it was cast in stone by an almighty being and all we had to do was to sit back, relax and watch it develop and flourish on its own.

He sends me birthday wishes every year. I never return the gesture when his birthday comes around. Just as I do—or don't—with other people I have gotten to know throughout life. Why is that?

Sometimes I want to hear from people but I never get my act together and write them. What would people think if they all of a sudden received a message from me? Why is this guy sending me something now? After all these silent years? Wouldn't I have to explain it somehow why I was writing now but not before? And if I wrote, wouldn't it create some sort of moral commitment on my behalf to keep up with regular writing? I'm not sure if I could withstand such a pressure.

In the end, I decided to send Jo birthday wishes this year. I really wanted to hear from him. Regardless of how it would look. Regardless of what he would think.

It wasn't easy. The economic situation in his part of the world is quite unstable these days, to say the least. Would he find it distasteful if I made a reference to it along with the birthday wishes? Would he find it a sign of ignorance and lack of empathy on my behalf if I didn't mention it at all?

What about news of me? Should I send some nuggets? He has hardly heard from me in what, three, four, five years. Time flies. Where did it go? Which news should I tell? The latest? The most exciting? Was there anything in my life that was newsworthy? Would he at all be interested in news from me? Wouldn't I just be wasting a few precious minutes of his day that he could make better use of celebrating his birthday?

In the end I just wrote him simple wishes. Nothing more. Just a happy birthday. Over and out.

Now it's almost midnight. Seven hours since I sent the message. He hasn't replied. Hasn't even opened the message.

Seems like I've messed it up. As I always seem to do.

North Of Nowhere

I sit by the window and peer into the darkness outside. The mighty mountain towers over our village like a monarch sitting on their throne, overlooking their land. I glance at the clock mounted high up on the wall, swinging its pendulum back and forth, patiently counting every second, while sending an endless stream of ticks and tocks through the otherwise silent living room. It's approaching mid-day and a flock of butterflies is released from a compartment within my stomach, flapping their tickling wings throughout my body. I return my eyes to the mountain, continuing the wait with my eyes fixed into the gloom.

It's tiring to stare into space without daring to blink, but I'm determined, certain my perseverance will pay off in the end. And it does. It happens. Suddenly. A small glimpse of light reaches over the mountaintop and glitters like the jewels on a royal crown. I watch the coronation of our monarch, mouth agape, struck by the beauty of the moment. The ceremony doesn't last long, though, and before I know it, the light has faded and left the narrow fjord draped in the same layer of shadows that has covered it for the past couple of months.

But dad had been right.

When I asked him back in December where the sun had gone, he said it had gone behind the mountain. When I asked him if it was ever coming back, he said matter-of-factly, yes, on January eighteenth, around mid-day. When I asked him why it had gone, he said it was because we lived at the end of the world—north of nowhere. His voice had sounded so sad that I didn't ask anything more and decided to wait, as patiently as I possibly could, for the new year to come and see for myself.

HONEST JOB

"Isn't it time to get yourself an honest job?"

I knew it was just an innocent question and that she didn't mean it in a bad way. She cared about me. She wanted to help me. She thought I needed help. Yet, the question irritated me. I interpreted her words as an echo of society's stereotypical condemnation of my lifestyle.

I felt like society could not tolerate that I worked intermittently as a contractor and in-between projects gave myself the time to think. Time to wander aimlessly about the streets of the city. Time to observe the world as it orbited around me.

Time to capture words I found on the beaten path, scribble them down in a notebook and arrange them into poetry.

I was perfectly aware that society pitied me for renting a small room in a former commercial building downtown, while it thought I easily had the potential to become a middle-manager in a large corporation and buy a house in one of the suburbs. Society felt I was squandering my talent by strolling quietly around the town instead of speeding in a Dodge RAM.

Society did not find it honest of me to refuse to do everything I possibly could in order to maximize gross national product. Foreign exchange earnings, man! Foreign exchange earnings! Society didn't think I paid enough taxes in order to finance the tax-breaks for the data-centers for mining cryptocurrency. It was appalled by the missed opportunity of green energy utilization resulting from my low power loitering.

Society had its expectations and I was not complying.

Screw society. I was happy.

Don't You Worry About A Thing

A chill ran down Jaime's spine as he sat at the kitchen table sipping his morning coffee before heading off to work. Through the window facing the back-garden, the pitch-black Arctic mid-winter darkness flowed into the small interior space and threatened to suffocate the ambient glow from the extractor fan above the cooktop. Jamie looked up from his coffee, to his left and to his right. Of course there was no one there. There never was.

Jamie listened to the footsteps in the hallway and felt someone breathing down the collar of his sweater. He turned around to face nothing but the static shadows that seemed to be permanently fixed to the place. Jaime shook his head—it was probably just the sound of the wind and the eternal darkness that was getting into his head.

It had been a month since Jaime moved to Iceland and rented a basement apartment in the center of Reykjavík. At first, he had been quite happy with the place. Albeit small, the flat was homely and decorated with care to make the tenant feel comfortable. However, as time went by the coziness had faded and Jaime started to get the funny feeling he was not the sole occupant of the space. He didn't believe in ghosts or other supernatural beings, but he couldn't shake off the sensation that there was some unexplained presence in the apartment. He had wanted to bring the issue up with the landlord who lived on the floor above him but was afraid she would think he was crazy. Maybe he was. Perhaps he was losing his mind while struggling to adapt to this novel, cold and dark part of the world.

Jaime finished his coffee in one large gulp, put on his coat, eased his feet into the boots, wrapped a scarf around his neck, put a knit cap on his head, threaded his fingers into the mittens, grabbed the keys and ran out into the cold February morning, almost knocking his landlord over in the process. She had been shoveling snow in the driveway.

"Good morning," the landlord greeted, smiling with her entire face, drawing attention to the red frost-bitten cheeks. "How are you? Everything ok in the apartment?"

"Morning... Yes... Everything is fine. The place is nice and quiet. And the bed... Very comfortable. I'm really happy."

"Good to hear. You just let me know if there is anything you don't like."

Jaime hesitated for a moment, staring down at his snow covered boots.

"Well... There's just one little thing...," he stuttered at last.

"Tell me," the landlord insisted, leaning forward and resting her weight on the large snow-shovel.

"Well... I know it must sound silly... I mean... It must be my imagination... I mean... It cannot be true... The thing is... I just have this funny feeling that I'm not alone in the apartment."

"Oh, yeah, that," the landlord replied, the smile fading from her face and her glance drifting toward the entrance to the basement flat. "I had a clairvoyant pay a visit to the basement a few years ago. She told me there was a family of four living there. The family had previously lived in a shed where my house is now. However, the shed had burned down together with its inhabitants shortly before the current neighborhood was built."

Jaime felt his muscles tighten, his mouth go dry and a knot starting to form in his stomach. He wasn't sure if he should feel happy or sad about having his implausible suspicion confirmed.

"But, don't you worry about a thing," the landlord continued, the smile returning to her face. "Apparently, they are all good souls."

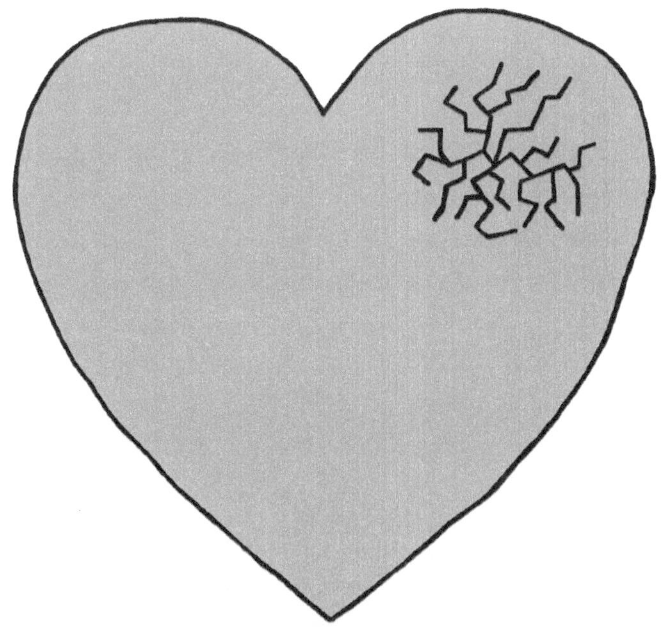

LOVE AT FIRST SIGHT

I looked up as you entered the café. Your hair fell over your
shoulders like a waterfall in a nature documentary. Or a sham-
poo commercial.

It was love at first sight.

You sat down at the table next to mine, took off your coat
and I admired your pink sweater. You looked up and our eyes
met. You smiled. I smiled back. We both looked away timidly.

It was dating at first sight.

Although you were pretty in pink, I imagined you yet more
stunning in white, as you walked down the aisle. Towards

me. Towards our merry matrimony. We would be so happy together.

It was marriage at first sight.

As you looked over the café, I took a sneak preview of your profile. Your nose would go well with my eyebrows. We would have beautifully symmetric children.

It was family at first sight.

You ordered a cup of coffee and brought it to your lips. I imagined you on our terrace in the suburbs, drinking coffee in the morning sun. We would get a puppy and call him Spencer.

It was dog at first sight.

And then, all of a sudden, you diverted your gaze toward the door. Your eyes lit up. You ran up to the man who had entered. A complete stranger. You embraced him. You engaged in a passionate kiss. How could you? How could you do this to me? To our relationship? To our beautifully symmetric children? To Spencer?

It was divorce at first sight.

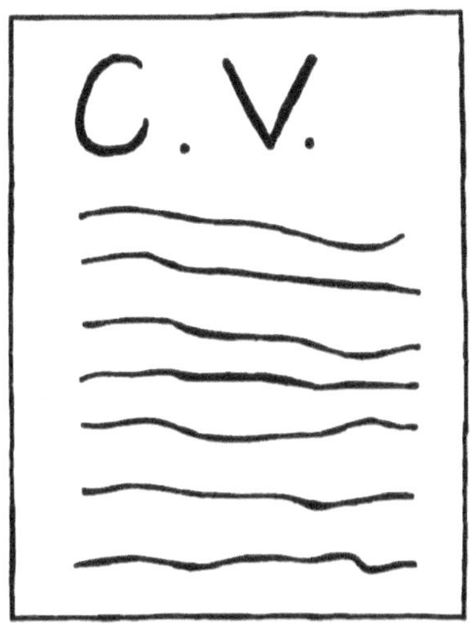

Answer Wanted, Maybe

I'm waiting anxiously for an answer. Fifty five hours have passed since I pressed the button and sent in my application for the role of team manager of the purchasing department. It was the job I had dreamt of landing for the past two years. Two years ago, the current team manager had told me she had already started counting down the days until she could retire. At that point the days were seven hundred thirty four.

For two years, I had prepared this moment. I had dili-gently observed every aspect of my superior's job. How she made decisions. How she treated the rest of us. How she organized the team's work.

Night after night, I had sat in my living room and written down a detailed job description for the role of team manager as it looked from my vantage point and how I would modify it when the role would finally end up in my hands. I wrote down how I would do things. What I would keep and what I would change. The result of the labor could be found in a hundred and twelve page Word document.

In parallel to my theoretical preparation I had also worked on practical matters. I had been eager to take on increased responsibility in my current role. Yet, I had been careful not to let my career ambition have a negative effect on my coworkers. I had treated everyone with respect and made a special effort to keep the team spirit high and made sure to make every team member's voice heard. As far as I could tell, I was liked by my coworkers and I had received encouragement from the boss who was glad to have less to do during the final stint of her career.

It was thus safe to say that I had been prepared when the job position had finally been advertised. I had thoroughly enjoyed preparing my application. I had been extremely excited and full of hope.

Now, when the application was out of my hands and in the hands of the company's general management, I had expected I would be feeling great. I had expected my excitement and hope to be extended.

I feel horrible. I cannot sleep. I cannot stop thinking about what would happen if—for some reason—I would not get the job. My heart jumps whenever I receive an email. I don't dare to look at it. What if it contained a negative answer? I avoid eye-contact with the chief executive of the company whenever I meet her in the corridors at work or in the cafeteria. I don't dare looking in her eyes in case they could potentially express any hint of me not getting the position.

I don't want an answer. I want to press pause. I want to continue living in my dream world where the dream job is undoubtedly mine.

SMALL TALK

I stood by the window and looked out as I sipped the thin coffee. Outside there was a snowstorm raging. Everything was white. I turned around and looked over the room. Some people were sitting down while others stood upright. Everyone was sipping their coffees and either looked down into their cup or into the air without saying anything. I felt this party was missing some small talk—something to liven up the atmosphere. Yet, I couldn't think of a subject that might raise the interest of people around here.

What was I doing here? That was easy to answer. I was learning to write poetry—in a course I had been given as a Christmas present by my parents. But what was I doing HERE? What was I doing in a community center in the rural part of Iceland in the middle of January? What was a high school student from Reykjavík doing at a poetry course with middle-aged farmers? Middle-aged was a flattering choice of phrasing in this context. What was the city-slicker doing in the countryside?

The course was actually good. It was working from the point of view my parents had intended. They had had enough of their son's contemporary poetry style that completely disregarded the rich Icelandic poetry heritage and wanted him to get to know the traditional structure and form. The heritage was definitely to be found in this countryside community center with post-middle-aged poetry loving farmers in a January snowstorm. To my surprise, I was enjoying myself and learning quite a lot.

The poems resulting form this course were diverse. I wrote under the influence from Lord Byron and Rousseau. The farmers wrote under the influence from Birgir the ram and Sólveig the sheep. Maybe I was exaggerating a bit the cultural difference between myself and the farmers. Over lunch I had learned that on a farm nearby, Hegel and Kierkegaard were chewing hay side by side and Augusta Ada Lovelace Byron had given birth to three lambs last summer. Despite my prejudgement, the farmers were no less knowledgeable of the classics than I was—on the contrary in some cases.

We were maybe not as different as I had imagined—the farmers and I. Weren't we connecting with each other through the poetry? Who knew if I could maybe make some coffee-break small talk around here? There had to be something I could think of saying. A couple of farmers had been talking about snow coverage a few moments ago. Now they were silent—like myself—staring into the blizzard raging outside. Wasn't that it? I could make a comment about how strong it was blowing today. Something like that. It would no doubt be a successful conversation starter around here.

"I guess this is what they call a snowstorm in Reykjavík," commented one of the farmers before I had been able to put my thought into words.

The other farmers laughed and then returned to their silence. I settled for an awkward smile. Maybe I wasn't ready yet to make small talk in this crowd.

Book Of Struggle

For as long as Morgan could remember, he had dreamt of telling the story of his struggle with chronic illness. He desperately wanted to write a book about how he had lived through decades of constant suffering—tell the tales of endless hospital visits, followed by lengthy periods of partial-recoveries, where time inched forward at a snail's pace with intolerable pain.

The work would not only describe the physical torment of long-term infirmity, but also shed a light on the mental stress and nagging uncertainty that constantly loomed over him and his closest family like a black storm cloud. He would open up about how his wife Belinda broke under the pressure of his sickness and how their marriage was torn apart in the process—leaving their innocent children, Matt and Mandy, split between multiple homes.

Last but not least, Morgan wanted to expose the malicious practices of a corrupt and immoral health care system where hard-working but feeble people like himself were metaphorically trodden into the ground and left to bleed to death in the streets while the capitalist elite was treated with the utmost care.

However—as fate would have it—the opportunity never presented itself for Morgan to make his dream come true. He was always as fit as a fiddle.

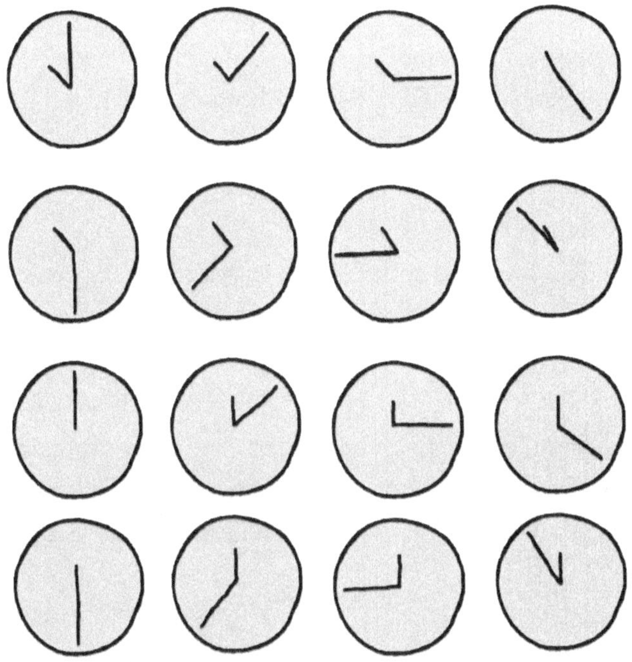

Second Sight

I looked at my watch. It was still two hours until I had an appointment with the representative of the publisher that was potentially interested in publishing my novel.

There were two weeks since I had had a short chat with her after the poetry reading of the writing group Small Matters. I had been quite proud when she came up to me after my reading and asked about my writing—if I wrote something besides poetry. I told her about the manuscript in my drawer and we decided to meet over a cup of coffee in a downtown café.

My mind wandered back to the poetry reading and I tried to remember what she had looked like—the representative of the publisher. I couldn't visualize her face. I had been quite elevated when we met. Both because of my debut poetry reading and because of the attention she had given me. The details were covered in fog.

What if I would not recognize her again? What if I entered the café, walked past her without recognizing her and sat down at a different table?

She would surely be offended. Wouldn't she just strike my name off the list of promising writers? My writing career would be over—before it took off. My career would crash at take-off—run out of gas before reaching the end of the runway.

★ ★ ★ ★ ★

I sat down with my cup of coffee and looked at my watch. It was still thirty minutes until our appointment. I was early. It was the best thing for me to do. This way I would not need to worry about not recognizing her. Now it was her responsibility to recognize me.

I looked again around me at the café. To be sure. I looked from one table to the next and focused on excluding the possibility that any of the guests could be the representative of the publisher. A man. Too old. A group of boys. Too young. Could this be her? No, she wouldn't have brought her child with her.

I was safe.

★ ★ ★ ★ ★

I watched the woman with the child as she left the café. The clock showed five minutes past. Had it been her? Could it be that she had had a problem with finding a babysitter and taken her child with her? It had been intended as an informal meeting anyway. Had my fear become reality? Had she left the café in anger because I had failed to recognize her? Had my inability to remember people's faces let me down once again?

★ ★ ★ ★ ★

As the woman with the child left the café, another woman entered—the representative of the publisher. I recognized her at once. How could I have doubted?

Bipartisan

I made myself comfortable on the sofa, reached for the remote control and turned on the television. Coming up, was a two-hour long soccer feast. A match between two national teams I had little connection to and could therefore enjoy the game without any emotional side effects.

The team in white started with the possession of the ball. After a few short and rapid passes in the midfield area, the ball reached one of the center backs who dribbled the ball casually while looking for a good pass upfield. This was a promising start.

The camera showed the player in close-up. It was someone who I recognized. He was a player for the arch rivals of my favorite team in the English league. I hadn't known that this was his national team.

The center back made a long pass up to the left wing where his teammate received the ball elegantly. The camera zoomed back in as the left winger tried to get past his opponent on his way up towards the corner flag. My heart skipped a beat. Him too. Were the center back and the left winger compatriots in addition to playing with the same league club? I couldn't believe my eyes.

These two players annoyed me when they played against my favorite league club. I found them to be arrogant. I couldn't tolerate them. I hated them. I couldn't be impartial anymore. As the game progressed I started to hate their compatriots. I started automatically to cheer for the other team. Their opponents. I got annoyed at the referee when he judged foul against my team. Yes, the opponents of my opponents were now my team.

I was in a somber mood when I stood up in half-time and went to grab a cold beer from the refrigerator. The game had been vivid. Both teams had managed to maintain good control over the ball and played rapid passes. They had created many opportunities in front of each of the goals and scored one a piece. On the other hand, I was stiff, my muscles were tense and I had an urge to hit doorposts with my fists. I felt that my team was losing.

When I opened the fridge, a light came on. Actually and metaphorically. The absurdity of the moment became clear in front of my eyes. By hating the players I had ruined for myself the relaxed and enjoyable moment the match had been supposed to give me. What was I thinking? I loathed myself. This couldn't be healthy. Neither for the body nor the soul—biologically nor existentially—neither for the individual nor for society as a whole. Something had to be changed.

While the players of both teams collected strength for the second half and experts in the studio discussed the first half, I walked in circles around the dining room table in order to calm my nerves and collect my thoughts. I became determined to combat this hatred that got hold of me so often when I was exposed to competitive sports. I decided that from now on I would stop discriminating between soccer teams. From now on I was going to cheer at each moment for the team that was in possession of the ball.

HUMAN MIRRORS

"I would never even contemplate going wandering about on my own," my co-worker said during our coffee break when we were discussing what we had been up to during the weekend and I mentioned my long solitary walk along the Amstel.

"Why not?" I asked, rather surprised by the idea. "It's not like there are many dangers lurking there on the riverbanks. Especially not in broad daylight."

"I'm not afraid," she said confidently. "I just don't want people to think I'm lonely."

"But are you?"

"What?"

"Lonely?"

"Of course not."

She was quick to change the subject and move our conversation into avenues related to our work. I reluctantly followed even if I felt we had much to discuss on this subject. I understood her point of view. I had once been in her shoes. Constantly mirroring myself in the eyes of others. Constantly worrying about not living up to the expectations of society regarding how people should or should not be. I had behaved myself in the manner I thought people expected me to behave.

That was then. Since, I had been able to divert my gaze into my own soul instead of continuously looking for the reflection of myself in the eyes of the people around me. It made me feel calm.

I promised myself I would one day try to help my colleague to look at the world in the same way. But not today. She wasn't in the right mood.

GRAVITY

Brendan felt gravity pull at his mind and body as he descended with the escalator, down into the dome between the subway platforms, staring into the void between scarcely lit concrete walls and feeling as if he were looking into a mirror of his own soul. His head was blank and nearly all physical energy had been drained from his body.

At the bottom of the stairs, he dragged his feet along the largely deserted platform, toward the opposite end where he sat down on a vacant bench. He wanted to keep as large a distance as possible between himself and the few passengers who were still about at this late hour.

Brendan wanted to be all alone. Alone with his thoughts. The stray images that kept jumping in and out of the black canvas that covered the back of his head. He tried, in vain, to pin the images down, arrange them into a complete picture—a collage of his hopeless situation.

It wasn't as if Brendan hadn't tried all he could. He had definitely tried. He had pitched. He had argued. He had pleaded. He had begged. Yet, all his efforts had been futile. The answers had been no, no and no. There was no more money to be had. No more patience. No more line of credit. He had lost all hope of being able to free himself from the knot he found himself tied in.

Brendan heard the train approaching. A faint glow lit up the dark opening of the tunnel. He stood up and walked over to the edge of the platform, so close that his weary body struggled to keep balance. The light at the tunnel mouth grew brighter. The noise became louder. A gentle breeze played with the locks of his hair as the headlights rushed toward him. He felt the pressure. He closed his eyes.

When Brendan opened his eyes again, the train had stopped and was standing by the platform with its doors ajar. He stepped in and let his body collapse into an empty seat. As things were standing, there wasn't much he could do. Nothing besides heading home and try to get a few hours of sleep before he had to go to the office in the morning, face his employees and tell them the hard truth—deliver them the bad news. Tell them that the company was bankrupt.

LIFE FLOWS ON

He sits on the edge and looks over the powerful river raging through the canyon beneath his feet. The force is undeniable. The water gets hurled from one canyon wall to the other as it makes its way towards the ocean. A few moments earlier he had looked over the stream higher up in the valley and admired how calm the flow had been in the broad waterway. The scene does not make him anxious. He knows that downstream the landscape will once again broaden, the river will spread out and the current will subside.

Time is water—life is a river.

Sometimes we make a decision to turn our life around. We set ourselves clear goals. Turn the tables to our advantage. We walk the path of life taking slow and steady steps. We move one foot in front of the other, take calm breaths and repeat. Then, all of a sudden, life takes us into a different direction. Without conferring with us. Without us having anything to say in the matter. We lose control. We are forced to go with the flow, using all our energy to keep our heads above water until we get a grip on our existence again and find a chance to get back up on our feet. An opportunity to direct our life back to the course through which we want it to flow.

BRILL

I strap on my running shoes as I so often do when I feel anxiety take over my thoughts. When I feel the doubt eating through my cerebral cortex. When foggy clouds cover my thoughts and obstruct my mental vision. When I don't know where I'm headed. When I don't know which foot to move first. Then I strap on my running shoes in order to force myself to systematically place one foot in front of the other without needing to think. One step at a time.

While running, I usually manage to get my thoughts under control. I try to get a better grasp of the problems I'm facing. They are normally of a similar sort—if not the same—all the time. No big changes, no big revelations, but it is good to refresh the memory. The running helps me visualize and organize the next baby-steps I can take towards a solution to my problems. I just need to place one foot in front of the other. And repeat.

On today's run none of that happens. The only thing that goes through my head is the song from the Brill margarine commercial. On repeat. How it is praised. How filling it is. How it nurtures. The same lines of lyrics over and over again from the time I leave the garden gate until I finish the last stretching exercise.

That's how it is sometimes. Sometimes you achieve what you set out to do. Sometimes not. I just need to accept it and move on.

THE BIG QUESTION

I followed her into the apartment, stepped over the threshold, passed a milestone, walked towards a new chapter in my life, a new future—who knew?

"Make yourself comfortable on the sofa while I prepare the tea."

I rubbed my hands together. I was cold. The cup of tea would help me recover my normal body temperature, and continue the disruption of the *status quo* that had characterized my life for so long—who knew?

We had met a couple of months ago in the stretching room of the gym and started talking. Our chat had kicked off on the subject of stretching but somehow we ended up talking about Alvar Aalto's influence on modern architecture. To this day, the exact conversation is a bit blurry in my mind—I'm not sure how we jumped from one subject to the next—but the important conclusion of the encounter was that we connected on some divine level.

After our first gym encounter I started to exercise more regularly. Although it was maybe not entirely a conscious decisions, I guess I did it in the hope I would run into her again.

Eventually I did. She was exercising on a treadmill by the big window overlooking the snowy lawn. I walked up to the machine next to hers and started running. While working out, we stole glances at each other and smiled. After a long run we nodded simultaneously and headed over to the stretching room where we continued our conversation where we had left it the other day.

Over the next few weeks we met regularly inside and outside the gym. We trained together. We took long walks. We went out for coffee. We continued talking. We covered one subject after another. I fell in love.

Today was the first time I had entered her apartment. This afternoon we had been walking in the woods for several hours in the freezing cold and she had suggested we rounded up the walk by going to her place for a cup of tea. I gladly accepted.

"I hope you like green tea," she said as she entered the living room with a teapot and two cups on a tray which she put down on the coffee table by the sofa. "It's the only tea I've got in the house."

"Yes, I like green tea."

I decided not to mention that it was actually my favorite type of tea. It would have sounded too cheesy. Too superficial. Too good to be true.

She poured the tea, handed me a cup and we immediately started our customary chit-chat, traversing quite fluidly as usual from one subject to the next without any effort. With a small exception, though. From my side the conversation was not as fluid as before. There was an elephant in the room I had to address. There was an important question on my mind. The big question.

She, however, continued talking as before—chatting about everything and nothing—jumping from one subject to the next. I tried my best to keep up with her, but in the background I couldn't stop thinking about how I could bring up my question, struggling to find a moment to sneak it in.

Then there came a brief silence while she poured us some more tea. This was my moment. This was my chance. I grabbed it.

"Could you ever consider owning a dog?"

Immediately after asking the questions I knew I didn't want to hear her answer. I was terrified to know what she thought.

"Yes," she said without hesitation. "One of these days I'll definitely get myself a big Labrador."

On that moment a dark cloud blocked the sunshine that had brightened up my life for the past few weeks. I knew it was all over. The relationship had no future.

THE FOREIGN CITY IS A BEAUTIFUL MAZE WE NAVIGATE IN THE SEARCH OF HIDDEN GEMS

I found myself a nice table in the shadow of a mature tree, sat down and admired the vibrant square—one of so many in the city I was gradually starting to call my home. The sky was clear and there was quite a crowd around in the Sunday morning sun—people of all ages, conversing seniors, teenagers engaged in acrobatics on a line that had been stretched between two trees, children running around and chasing pigeons under observant parental eyes.

A waiter came over to the table and I nearly exhausted all my knowledge of the local language by ordering myself a latte. When my drink arrived, I opened the book I had bought from the bookshop on the opposite corner of the square. I stared at the page in front of me, transforming the unfamiliar words into yet stranger sounds in my head, without being able to associate any meaning to what I was reading. There were so many foreign aspects to my life these days—the weather, the names, the customs, the language...

"Blah blah ... Blah blah blah ... blah?"

I looked up from my book and viewed the woman who had addressed me in the tongue of the natives. I had not understood a word of what she had said, but by the tone of her voice I guessed it had been a question.

"Sorry, I don't speak the language," I replied in the *lingua franca* I hoped she would understand.

"I see. I just asked if this chair was free."

"Oh. Yes. Go ahead."

Contrary to my expectations, she did not grab the chair and bring it to an adjacent table but sat down at mine. I smiled awkwardly in order to hide my surprise. I wasn't sure if I should get back to reading or if she expected my attention, so I just stared at her while she turned around in her chair, called a waiter and, if I was not mistaken, ordered an espresso.

"Interesting read?" She nodded toward the book I still had open in front of me.

"Well..." I wasn't sure how to respond.

"So, you can read our language but not speak it?"

"Actually... yes... the reading is not that much of a problem... it's the understanding that is more complicated."

"Let me see," she said, reaching out for the book. *"The foreign city is a beautiful maze we navigate in the search of hidden gems,"*
she read out loud. "That's what the first sentence says."

"Thanks," I said as she handed the book back to me. I
reached for a pen and scribbled the translation at the top of
the page. That should help me get started with deciphering
the remaining text.

"You're welcome!" She downed in one gulp the espresso
the waiter had put in front of her, put a few coins on the table,
stood up and disappeared into the crowd at the busy square.

Elf Betrayal

"The Icelandic belief in elves is nothing but a pile of utter nonsense," claimed my grandmother where we sat in the dining area of her residency and played a game of chess.

"How come?" I asked, a little surprised by her comment, which I found to come out of thin air. "Why do you say that?"

"When I was young," my grandmother started her story using the same phrase as she so often used in her later years. "I was sent to herd the cows in the field every afternoon. Every single day I had to walk past the big lava field that was famous for being the habitat of elves. Every time I passed the elfish colony I spoke to the elves and made a wish I would become a poet."

My grandmother paused her story while she killed one of my pawns with her bishop and threatened my king.

"And how did life turn out?" she continued after the killing. "I moved to Reykjavík, studied law, founded my own practice and ended up as a supreme court judge."

She paused her story again, looked up from the chess table and out of the window.

"But I never became a poet."

This piece of flash fiction is based on a true story.

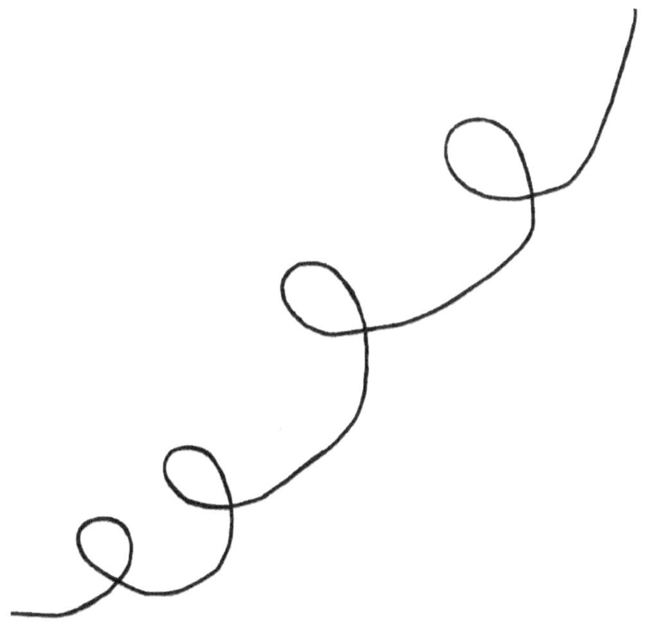

Floss

I was abnormally excited about seeing the dentist today. I was looking forward to the visit. Throughout my life the sensation had usually been the exact opposite. I had dreaded the visits rather than looked forward to them. My main anxiety was invariably related to the inevitable theme of flossing. That is, the statutory time-point in the session when the dentist asked "But, how is it? Do you floss every day?" I was always forced to shamefully admit that I was an irregular flosser. It seemed to be absolutely impossible for me to maintain the habit of regularly passing a dental floss between my teeth.

Now, my life's plot had taken a twist. For a year—367 days to be exact—there had not passed a single day without me flossing my teeth. I was immensely proud of myself and full of self assurance about being able to face up to the dentist and leave his practice without the feeling of shame and incompetence.

★ ★ ★ ★ ★

"Well," said the dentist as he finished his inspection. "This mouth looks to be caries free."

I was all smiles. This sounded promising.

"But, how is it?" the dentist continued and I was excited to finally be able to reply positively to the question that I was expecting to follow. "Don't you drink a bit too much coffee? Your teeth are terribly stained."

The smile disappeared from my lips and I was about to cry out "But I floss daily." It would futile, though. It seemed quite impossible to please these damn dentists.

Stop Talking To Yourself

"Stop talking to yourself!"

I looked over to the sofa where my sister lay on her back with an open book in her lap and a pen in her hand. She shot me a grim look that was no-doubt meant to follow her words through, deep under my skin and into the soul. Her words had no impact on me. They ricocheted off me like waves falling onto a well polished rock.

"I'm not talking to myself," I replied. "Not out loud, at least."

"Maybe not out loud in the literal meaning of the words," she admitted. "But the body language you express as you pace the room makes it quite clear that you are talking to yourself. And, in fact, at the top of your voice. Quite deafening. I must say."

"And what if I'm talking to myself?" I asked and paused my circling of the dining room table so I could better concentrate on the discussion.

"It's creepy," she uttered before pausing a second to blow a bubble with her gum. "Why can't you be normal?"

Normal. What was that, now?

"And what do you think you are doing?" I asked back, rolling my eyes.

"What does it look like?" she asked and lifted the book she had been writing in before. "I'm writing in my journal. That is, when I'm able to concentrate in-between your silent screams."

"Can I read?"

"No."

"Can anyone read?"

"No," she replied and quickly closed her book as a precaution and to underline her words. "It's my journal and no one reads it but me."

"Aren't you then just as much talking to yourself as I'm talking to myself?" I asked and continued my journey around the living room table, taking good care to step down correctly so that my feet matched the pattern in the underlying carpet.

"We're definitely not the same," she sighed. "It's normal to write a journal but it's not normal to talk to yourself. Why don't you just keep a journal like other civilized people?"

She opened her journal again and prepared to go back to her writing. I gave myself time to reflect on how I could reply. Right foot with a five degree outward angle. Left foot with a five degree inward angle.

"I don't want to," I said finally, after a few seconds contemplation. "I don't like to leave a paper-trail. It's also more environmentally sustainable to talk to yourself. Lower carbon footprint."

"How was the shower?" you asked as I came out of the bathroom with a towel wrapped around my waist and walked over to the bed which was situated in one corner of the studio apartment we had checked into a few hours earlier—a spacious holiday rental, above the workshop of a Danish painter, inland from the northern part of the Gothenburg archipelago. I looked over to you where you sat in an armchair by the window in an opposite corner of the space, looking comfortable with a blanket wrapped around your shoulders, an open book in your lap, and staring out the window into the Scandinavian autumn dusk.

"Good," I replied, hesitating for a while, reflecting on the fact that there had been something odd about my showering experience, something I had not consciously registered until you asked me about it.

"The pressure was fine, I guess," I continued, thinking out loud. "In fact, the shower was really powerful, when I think about it. But there was something about the smell of the water. It was strange—somehow. A bit metallic. Like blood. Probably due to the mineral composition of the bedrock around here."

"Powerful bloodbath?" you asked, turning your head from the window and into my direction. "That sounds bit scary. A Nordic Noir kind of vibe."

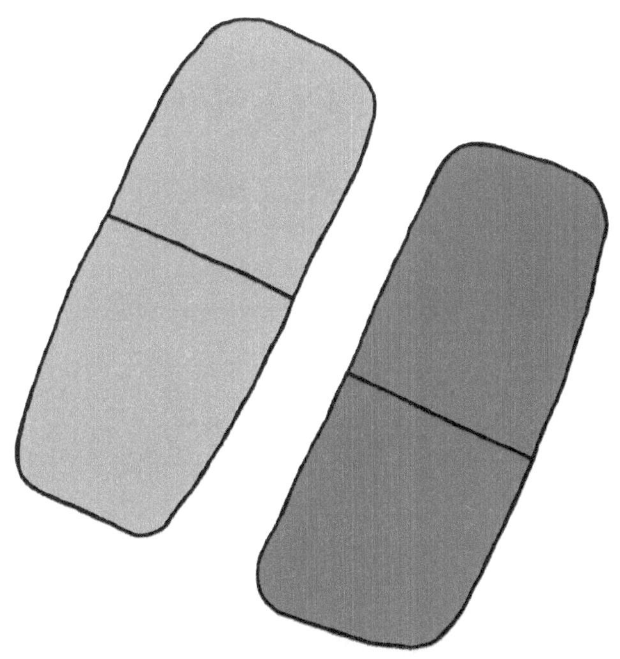

Pink And Purple

"Well," said the doctor as he bent his head over his desk and scribbled on a piece of paper. "I'm going to prescribe two types of pills for you. You'll take the pink ones every night to help you sleep and the purple ones you can take whenever you feel that you are becoming overwhelmed with the worries that tend to lead you to your panic attacks."

"But," I stuttered. "Can't you prescribe anything that could address the root cause of my problems? Something that could eliminate the anxiety? Can't you prescribe social justice? Universal basic income? Love towards fellow beings? Prejudice free society? Gender equality? Environmental responsibility?"

The doctor stopped scribbling, raised his gaze and looked me in the eyes.

"No, my friend," he answered, shaking his head ever so slightly.

"But don't you worry about a thing," he continued as he looked down again and went back to writing my prescription. "Just be diligent in taking those pills and they'll make you forget all those other things that you mentioned."

One Way Or The Other

"Isn't life such a dream nowadays," commented a small toucan rhetorically to a larger one as they sat on a branch of a genip tree, baking themselves in the early morning sun, after having stuffed themselves with large quantities of the delicious genipap fruit. "I mean, now with the humans gone, everything is so much quieter, so much safer. You can feel the air is fresher when it gently touches your beak as it moves about the wetlands. We've seen an end to all that inhumane human destruction. The deforestation has come to a halt. The climate catastrophe has conveniently eliminated the species that caused it. It's like true nature has returned."

"I must say I don't see the world as lyrically as you do," the larger toucan replied in its usual calm and melancholic voice. "I don't see that the is an awful lot of difference."

"No? How come?"

"You see that jaguar down there among the lower branches?" the larger toucan asked calmly without any discernible change in tone. "Carefully making its way toward us?"

"My god, yes," shrieked the smaller bird, letting go of the branch, hovering up in the air and flying over to the crown of the next tree, where it settled down again.

"Well," said the the larger toucan after joining the smaller one at its new location. "Next time, it's not that unlikely you won't. You'll be an easy prey for that hungry cat."

The smaller bird did not reply, remained uncharacteristically silent, staring into the distance.

"One way or the other," the larger toucan continued. "Humans or no humans. It's all the same. We eat. We are eaten. That's true nature for you."

TRIGGER

It was one of those moments when you put down whatever you have in your hands—in your case the book you had just finished reading—and start to cry without any apparent reason. You didn't sob out loud, but a seemingly endless stream of tears ran down your cheeks and fell onto the devil's ivy on the windowsill as you gazed out the open window—your stare fixed on the horizon without looking at anything in particular.

You weren't crying for the main character of the book who had, on the penultimate page, been tragically killed in a collision with a ten-ton truck while riding her bicycle home to her

soon to become—yet never ever becoming—loving husband.
You weren't thinking of them. You weren't thinking of her.
You weren't thinking of him.

You were thinking of him. He who had been such a good
friend and you had loved so profoundly. He who had battled so
hard for his life, but in the end, had been overcome by darker
forces and pulled out of this world, way before he was due.

You were thinking of her. She who was still of this world.
She who you also loved deeply. She who was so close—but yet
so far away. She whose heart remained out of reach of your
Cupid's arrows.

You weren't crying for any fictional characters. Your tears
were real. Tears of this world. Not just some drops of ink on
the pages of a printed book.

Matt Berg

"How did you like it?" my colleague asked as I handed him the novel I had borrowed from him a couple of weeks earlier.

"Pretty good", I replied and wasn't exaggerating. I had enjoyed the book very much.

"Wasn't it!"

"Indeed. In particular I found the character development to be good. They were so alive somehow—the characters. So believable. As if one knew them in real life."

"Yeah, exactly," my colleague agreed. "I experienced that too. I was able to immerse myself in the scene. I felt somehow as if I was a part of that group of friends in the story."

"I found the Matt Berg character especially realistic and convincing—somehow." I added. "I could visualize him so clearly in min mind."

"Matt Berg?" my colleague asked and we were clearly not on the same page.

"Yeah, the social scientist," I said to help him refresh his memory.

My colleague lifted his eyebrows. He then narrowed his eyes as if he wanted to dig into my mind to understand better what I was talking about.

"The ambitious one," I continued. "The dude who was thought to be so promising and clever but turned out to be an arrogant, hollow and narcissistic idiot."

"Oh, that guy," said the colleague and was visibly relieved. "You mean Ollie Smith?"

"Ollie Smith?" I asked surprised. Now it was I who was not on the right page. "Was that his name?"

"Yes, most definitely," answered my colleague, with total conviction. "How could you misread the name in such a way? It's not as if the names rhyme or have any resemblance whatsoever."

"No clue," I answered, shrugged my shoulders and looked out of the window. I visualized the face of the character who had been so particularly realistic when I read the book. I saw the grinning image of Matthew Steinberger. Matt Berg. My ex-classmate who had so often made attempts to humiliate me in high-school all those years ago. Had tried to cast doubt upon my abilities. Had tried to promote his own work by attempting to make mine look dodgy.

There at that moment I saw his image clearly in my mind. I who had all but forgotten his existence.

9TH FLOOR

"This hotel is quite an experience," said David, wide awake, staring into the empty darkness above the bed.

"Uhm," murmured Carmen, somewhere from the land between sleep and consciousness.

"I mean, I don't think I've ever slept so high up. Ninth floor, man. Ninth floor."

"Yeah, that's high."

"Isn't it amazing that you can feel the altitude, even if you're not even looking out the window. You just feel it. It's there in your body, your bones, your guts. That high riding feeling. It's just there."

"Amazing."

"I mean, what is it? What makes you feel the altitude? Is it because you know you're high up and have seen the views before and the mind just paints the picture on the back of your eyelids? Or is it gravity? Because it's so strong up here? Or maybe because it's weak? I don't know. Could also be sounds. I mean, you can hear the sounds coming from far below. Really far below. The sound-waves hit your eardrums at a narrow angle and the brain says wow, that's a really narrow angle and therefore the sound must be coming from really far below. I don't know. Could it be a combination of all these things? I don't even know if it is psychological or physical. Or some kind of a weird psycho-physical mixed-reality experience."

"Whatever. Can we talk about it in the morning? I'm kind of tired."

"Sure," said David, reluctantly letting go of the subject, silently continuing the dialog in his own head, though, concentrating intensely on his sensations, feeling the altitude, feeling the gravity, being bedazzled, listening to the sounds from far below, hitting his eardrums at an unfamiliar angle, fascinating angle, keeping him wide awake, blowing his mind, causing him to go on thinking in circles, about the wonders of altitude, gravity, trigonometry, psychology, physics, and gravity again, all in circles, until finally, in the early hours, also becoming tired, falling asleep, just to wake up a few hours later, on the ninth floor, without feeling anything, just waking up in a hotel room like any other.

Twenty Twenty

I looked both ways before stepping out into the street. I listened for footsteps. The coast was clear. No one was around. I could leave the house.

I had barely taken two steps down the road when I heard the helicopter hovering above my head, repeating the same message over and over again.

"WE'RE IN A MEDICAL EMERGENCY... STAY AT HOME... DON'T PUT OTHER PEOPLE AT RISK... STAY AT HOME... WE'RE IN A LOCKDOWN... STAY AT HOME..."

I hid under the canopy of a large tree while the chopper passed, hugging the trunk, trembling in tune with the leaves above me. Had they seen me? Did they know where I was going? Could they read my mind? Had they reported me? Would someone come for me? Take me away? Was I in trouble?

"WE'RE IN A MEDICAL EMERGENCY... STAY AT HOME... DON'T PUT OTHER PEOPLE AT RISK... STAY AT HOME... WE'RE IN A LOCKDOWN... STAY AT HOME..."

Gradually the message faded until it was just a murmur in the distance and an echo in my head.

"WE'RE... STAY... DON'T... STAY... WE'RE... STAY..."

I let go of the tree and continued my journey down the street. My body remained stiff and my heart pounded in my chest. What was I venturing into?

As I reached the main street I noticed there were some more people around. Scattered over the two sidewalks, keeping their distance. Some walking along the middle of the road. I could feel their gaze turn towards me as I took my place among them, keeping my distance, like a delicate product passing along on a slow moving conveyor belt. I could feel their thoughts penetrating my head.

"What's he doing here? How dare he? Has he no shame? No respect for others?"

I bowed my head, looking down at my feet, as I took my carefully choreographed steps along the sidewalk, keeping my distance. I made myself as small as possible. Kept my arms tight to my sides. On one hand I wanted to become invisible, escape the inquisitive eyes of my neighbors. On the other, I wanted to shout. I wanted to come clean.

"I DON'T MEAN YOU HARM. I'M NOT HERE TO HURT YOU. I'M JUST GOING SHOPPING. I'M OUT OF FOOD."

Reckless Behavior

"So... I'm boring... too predictable... too prudent... too..." Murray shouted after Lynn as she slammed the door behind her and left the house. "I'll show you recklessness... spontaneity... I'll show you..."

Murray was angry—really angry. He and Lynn had been arguing once again—if their interaction could be called an argument, that is. The whole episode was more like a one-sided rant from Lynn about how bored she was living with him— how fed-up she was of his pragmatic and systematic approach to life. She said she needed someone who was more daring—

someone more spontaneous—someone more human. That's what she had said. She wanted to be with someone more human.

Murray felt the tension build up in his body. He felt the urge to do something wild—let everything loose. He strode from one room to the other, thinking about what he could do. He looked about himself, seeking an object on which he could focus his anger—object onto which he could release the tension.

In the bathroom Murray spotted the toothpaste tube and crazy ideas started to form in his head. You can do it, he convinced himself. You are not as boring as Lynn says. You can be rash. You can be daring. Yes, you can. Murray grabbed the toothpaste tube from the bathroom shelf and squeezed it in the middle.

"See!" Murray shouted at the void Lynn had left in the apartment when she ran out. "See what I can do... I can be laid-back... I can be impetuous... Not everything needs to be optimized."

Murray put the toothpaste tube back onto the shelf, sat down on the toilet seat and tears started flowing down his cheeks. At first, he felt relieved. Then, he felt exhausted. He felt the tension in his body gradually subside and he started to calm down. He sat for a minute or two staring at the bathroom floor, before looking again up at the toothpaste tube where it sat on its shelf. This wasn't right. What kind of a man had he become? This wasn't the life he wanted to lead.

Murray stood up, walked over to the shelf and squeezed the toothpaste tube from the top to bottom—like one should do.

I sensed a strong scent of perfume when I stepped into the hall-way. It disturbed me. I got all tense. It was as if I had walked into a wall. Literally into the middle of a wall. Freshly poured concrete wall. The wet and viscous concrete surrounded me and held me tight in a straitjacket. I couldn't move. I couldn't breathe. The dense perfume smelling concrete thrust its way into my nose and down to my lungs.

I waved my hands in the air, managed to break loose from the casting mold and practically flew down the stairs. Upon reaching the bottom, I flung the front door open and jumped onto the sidewalk. Out into the fresh air. Out of the shackles forced on me by the perfume smell. Out into freedom. I danced in circles on the sidewalk with my arms spread out and stretching my head towards the endless clear blue sky.

Having caught my breath again, I stopped the carousel, looked straight ahead and started walking towards the ocean. A stroll along the coast was what I needed at the moment. I needed to gaze at the sea and admire the waves as they threw themselves over the beach, retreated and returned. Rhythmically and predictably.

Life was so weird these days. There was so much to think about. There was so much to understand.

"I suggest we explore where you are on the autism spectrum," the psychologist had said.

That was the task of the moment. To break this simple sentence up into its constituent atoms and puzzle it back together taking into account everything I had heard, seen and sensed during the entire forty-six years I had been breathing on this earth.

Smell was one of the sensations that occupied my mind these days. I could not remember having ever felt the smell of perfume as so invasive. These days I could not stand it. This sudden intolerance was so weird. Yet it felt somehow so natural.

What was the explanation? Was I finally allowing myself to connect with my own sense of smell rather than just accepting blankly that this was how normal people smelt like? Had I stopped mirroring my own sense of smell in the sense of smell that was simplest to have so I could seamlessly integrate with my surrounding?

My answer was yes. Yes, I had started to smell what I really smelt rather than smelling what I assumed society expected me to smell.

I breathed deeply in through the nose and devoured the smell of the sea. Yummy. This was a smell I liked. It felt liberating.

"What is it with you and dogs?" my friend asked as we sat in the glistering sun, drinking iced-coffee and looking over the square.

"What do you mean?" I snapped back as the question had hit me off-guard and I had no clue where he was going with this dialog. Dogs weren't really my thing.

"Did a dog bite you as a child?"

"No," not that I could remember.

"Did you own a dearly loved dog that met its fate in a tragic accident?"

"No," I would have remembered if that had been the case.

"Did you always want a dog but were never allowed to?"

"No," pets had never been high on my wish lists.

"Why do dogs then always appear in such a negative light in your stories?"

"What?" They do?

In my mind I ran through the collection of short stories I had published a few weeks earlier. Dogs did indeed make an appearance in a few of the stories, but I couldn't see that they did so in a negative way.

"It's like there's a dog in your soul," my friend declared after a short pause.

That was the weirdest psychoanalysis I had ever heard.

"I must say that I neither believe in a dog in a soul nor a soul in a dog." This was a funny phrase. Something I could use in a story at some point.

"Look! You did it again!"

"What?" Now I was completely lost in this discussion.

"Oh, never mind," my friend sighed. "I would, however, if I were you, have this issue looked at by a specialist one day."

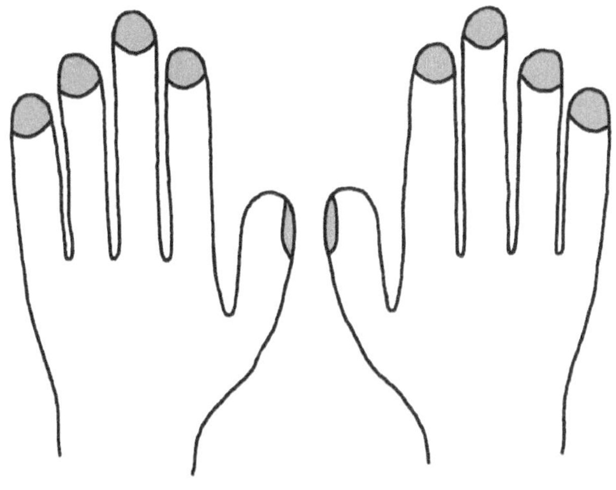

HANDWRITINGS

I splashed cold water in my face to refresh myself after a long night's sleep. The fingertips caressed the skin as they slid from the forehead to the chin. I opened my eyes and could feel my body come to life.

I looked down at the hands and felt as if I didn't recognize them—pale, thin and veinous. Could it be the same pair of hands that had served me so well throughout the decades? The hands that had worked long days at the carpentry workshop and written so many poems on long dark winter nights.

I sat down at my desk, grabbed a pen in one hand and used the other to hold still the sheet of paper. The words flowed from the pen and a new stanza line appeared after another. I definitely recognized the handwriting and the poetry style was the same as I had developed over the years.

They were most likely my own hands after all.

"Would you care to explain to me how this box of Ferrero Rocher chocolates ended up in your pocket?" the security guard hurled at me as I sat motionless with my hands in my lap on an uncomfortable wooden stool in the corner of his office. His voice was partially muffled by the resistance the sound-waves struggled to overcome on their journey through the thick fabric of the high-end face-mask covering the lower part of his face, no-doubt reducing the dramatic impact he had intended his speech to have on me—not unlike the effect of a gunshot silenced by a feathery pillow, as we so often see in the movies, I assumed. "Do you realize that shoplifting is not merely a crime against this very fine retail establishment? It certainly is not. It's a crime against society as a whole. It's an attack on the core values of our civilization. Trust. It's people like you who erode the trust between the human beings in this world."

I just looked up at him and shrugged without giving any verbal reply. I had nothing to add to his philosophical analysis of humanity and its interactions. There was no point. He wouldn't understand me anyway. They never do—his types. Or any other type, for that matter. He wouldn't understand that from my point of view—from my philosophical standpoint, if he wanted to take the discourse to that level—my acts were not aimed against society. Quite on the contrary. One could clearly see them as being caused by society. It was not me who was mistreating the code of our civilization. It were the norms of this said civilization that were mistreating me—putting me into an awkward situation.

Had the world not demanded of me to put on a face mask before entering the supermarket, it would not have ignited in my head the stereotypical scene from the movies where the bank robber puts on a balaclava to cover their face before entering a bank. And whenever a cause rears its head, effect is bound to follow. Just ask Anton Chekhov—although he would rightfully accuse you of misquoting him. The point is that the whole episode was out of my control. It was society, with its norms and values, that made me feel like a bank robber. And when society makes me feel like a bank robber, I feel like robbing a bank. And if not a bank, then at least a box of chocolates. It's just as simple as that. But I knew he wouldn't get it.

Till Morning

I close my eyes and take a deep breath through my mouth. My nose is blocked. I have a heavy sensation in the chest and my throat is swollen. The incoming air irritates my lungs and I cough. I feel a dense fog in my head and know that the fever hasn't passed. The flu is still there.

The good news is that I know how to cure myself. I know the magic medicine. It's not complicated. All I need to do is to sleep. Rest. Give my body the space it needs to work itself through this flu—in its own natural way.

★ ★ ★ ★ ★

I open my eyes and look at the clock. It is still relatively early. Good. There is hope. I turn on my side, draw my knees to my chest and huddle into a fetal position.

Now I just need to use the opportunity I have to turn the tables. I need to reinforce the right mindset. Don't repeat what I have done over the past few days. Don't wake up with a profound sense of self-reproach over not having executed the tasks I had set my self to complete for work. Don't cry over the lost work hours. Don't panic even if all my plans have gone south. Now, I need to sleep to be able to rid my body of this invasive virus. I need to wrestle back the control over my own existence. Therefore I went to bed early. To be able to sleep. To let my body recover. Come on. I can do it.

★ ★ ★ ★ ★

I turn and lie on my back. The mental fog moves to the back of my head. I turn on my side. The fog moves into the forehead. It doesn't matter how much I twist and turn. I can't find a relaxing position. The brain fog amplifies. The knot in my stomach tightens.

If I don't fall asleep now, tomorrow will be the same disaster as the other three days I have wasted on this stupid sickness this week. I will wake up at nine, exhausted and full of guilt. I will go out of bed anyway and try to get some work done in order not to fall even further behind of my plans. I will convince myself I'm sufficiently recovered to work. I will argue that I'm not sick enough to justify wasting the day in bed. Just because I refuse to acknowledge that I'm not well enough. I will get little done because my head will be heavy and the eyelids heavier yet. As the day goes by my greatest achievement will be to aggravate my ailment without making hardly any progress towards my desired outcomes.

Unless. Perhaps I'll manage to fall asleep sometime soon. Don't panic. Just sleep.

★ ★ ★ ★ ★

I open my eyes and look at the alarm clock. Zero, zero, zero. Midnight. I let my head fall back onto the pillow.

I'm not coping. I need to get some sleep. I'm wide awake. I need to stop worrying about not recovering soon enough. The anxiety has taken control over my mind. I need to use the night to relax and rest the body. I feel the tension in every muscle.

★ ★ ★ ★ ★

I raise myself up in bed, grab some tissue and blow my nose. It's always the same story. Over and over again. I always tell myself that next time it will be different. The next time I will relax and allow my body to be sick. I will allow myself to sleep. I will allow my body to work itself through the infection at its own natural and efficient pace. Yet, when next time comes around I never allow myself to become sick. I toil on without getting anything done. I don't allow myself to sleep all day. I don't allow myself to recover.

★ ★ ★ ★ ★

I throw the duvet aside and grab my head in my hands. I cannot tolerate this flu anymore. It's so sad that I know how to get better. I just need to sleep.

Now my thoughts have reached yet another full circle without discovering anything I didn't already know. The only progress that has been made is for time to progress on its way from the beginning towards the end. It's fast approaching two o'clock. I'm still not sleeping. It isn't happening. I'm not going to sleep anytime soon. I'm not going to be fresh in the morning. The entire week is ruined.

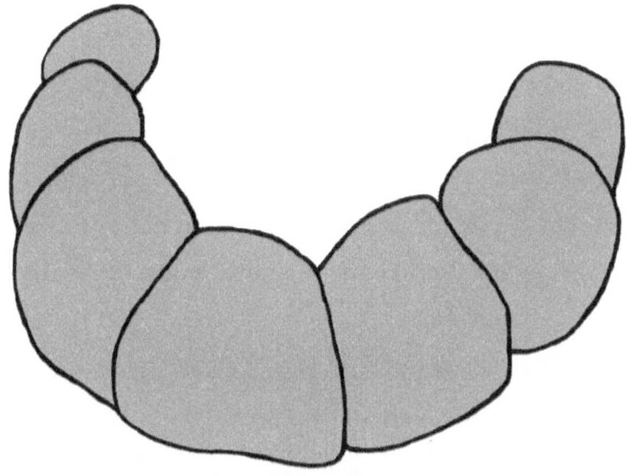

Oui

I sat down at a nice looking café to have breakfast. Tomorrow I was to give a conference presentation about graph theory but today I was going to ramble about the streets of Paris and get to know what the city had to offer. I did not have any particular itinerary planned. I was simply going to go on a random walk along the city's street network and see where my feet would take me. The only thing I knew for certain was that I had decided to try not to behave like a tourist. I was going to blend seamlessly into the crowd as if I were a local.

A waiter came over to my table and asked what he could offer me. I pronounced the sentence I had repeated constantly in my mind since opening my eyes this morning.

"Croissant et café au lait," I said as confident as I possibly could. Nevertheless the sentence did not sound quite as good when I said it out loud as it had done in my mind all morning. The intonation was different. Stiffer. Out loud, the words flowed like a pile of rocks falling off the back of a truck in pouring rain, but not like the calm brook on a sunny day I had imagined all morning.

"Un croissant et un café crême," the waiter murmured as he dutifully wrote down my order in a small notebook.

Rather than walking away from the table and into the kitchen to prepare my order, the waiter stood at my table and poured over me a river of french words whose meaning was completely beyond my level of comprehension. It had not been part of the scene I had imagined all morning that the ordering process would include anything beyond a simple request and an unconditional execution. Now I had to stay strong and don't admit defeat. I couldn't give up. I couldn't lose the cool. I had to imagine how a proper Parisian would react.

"Oui," I said casually when the waiter finally stopped talking.

The waiter nodded, smiled and walked over to the kitchen. I had to admit to myself that it could be a challenge to try to behave like a local without knowing hardly any french. Was I perhaps getting myself into trouble? What could it possibly have been that I had said yes to? It could hardly be anything serious, though, since the waiter had taken my answer as if it had been quite expected. I could therefore relax again and turn to my premeditated plan.

I observed the people in the street and tried to find something in their conduct that I could imitate in order to fool people into thinking I was a local. A quick observation revealed two aspects that were noteworthy about the Parisians. They smoked cigarettes and walked across the street against a red traffic light. I decided to pass up on the smoking but I was determined that on my rambling along the city streets I was not going to wait for a green light if the traffic allowed me to cross.

It wasn't long until the waiter returned and put a cup of milky coffee and a croissant on the table in front of me. The breakfast looked exactly as I had imagined it. My yes to the waiter's oration did not seem to have done any damage—whatever it had been I had said yes to. I decided not to dwell on that thought any longer. I would just have to accept my fate and go through the rest of my life without ever knowing what the waiter had said.

Life As It Should Be

She walked along the pothole filled gravel road, deep into the valley. The sun shone high in the sky and not a straw stirred in the perfect stillness. The majestic mountains rose above the fields and along the valley floor the river rattled like a snake. The water rushing forward, eager to make its way towards the deep ocean. Babbling brooks flowed down the slopes on both sides of the river until they merged into the bustling stream.

He walked along the pavement at the edge of the broad avenue leading to the main square. The sun filled the street with divine light and not a hair fluttered in the perfect calm.

On both sides of the thoroughfare tall buildings reared their towers into the blue sky, and along the street there was a constant flow of pedestrians on their way to the subway station. Even more people flowed from the buildings and side streets and merged into the sea of commuters.

She listened to the burbling river, the bleating sheep and the tweeting birds. Familiar languages that all merged into one whole. The language of nature. Familiar. Easily understood.

He listened to the murmur of the people, muffling teenagers, loud tourists and decorous office workers. Strange languages that merged into one whole. Foreign. Hard to decipher.

She left the road behind and strolled down the hill towards the floor of the valley. She enjoyed being in nature. To her, the scenery was like a flock of living souls. She looked from a hummock to a rock—from a rock to a hummock. She greeted a moss bearded boulder and asked if it was lonely in its old age. She addressed a tousled knoll and asked if it wasn't wonderful to grow up in the glimmering sun.

He moved away from the edge of the street and into the center, allowing himself to float with the sea of people towards the square. He enjoyed being alone in the crowd. To him, the people were a part of the scenery. He looked at the faces of the commuters breaking their way against the flow. He looked into the serious face of a middle-aged man who's sole concern seemed to be focused on getting to the next destination in life. He looked into the smiling face of a teenage girl who spoke joyfully into the air and a handsfree headset.

She felt as if she was surrounded by hustle and bustle—embroidered into the natural fabric that resonated with mutual recognition and formed a whole. She loved being caught in the vortex of nature.

He felt as if he was alone in the world—isolated from the people around him who barely registered his existence. He loved his solitary stroll through the sterile swarm of souls.

They looked at the road ahead, smiled and thought—she out loud and he to himself—this is life as it should be.

Börkur Sigurbjörnsson is a wandering body and mind who captures his world view in pieces of short fiction. He is a mathematician, logician and computer scientist by training but his interests cover a wide spectrum—from geology to politics, sociology, business innovation, and urban planning. This generalist view of the world is reflected in the wide range of topics covered in his stories. Börkur was born in Reykjavík, Iceland, but has over the past decades lived in various places around Europe and South America with prolonged says in Amsterdam, Barcelona, Burscheid, Düsseldorf, London, Montevideo and Paris. While many of Börkur's stories are written from a quirky introvert perspective, they reflect his exposure to a variety of distinct cultures.

Among Other Things is Börkur's fourth short fiction publication. Previously he has published the short story collections *999 Abroad* (2012) and *Talk to Strangers* (2019) as well as the flash fiction collection *Flash 52* (2017).

Börkur regularly publishes flash fiction and short stories on his website, *Urban Volcano*.

www.ingramcontent.com/pod-product-compliance
Lightning Source LLC
Chambersburg PA
CBHW031153160726
47992CB00006B/2431